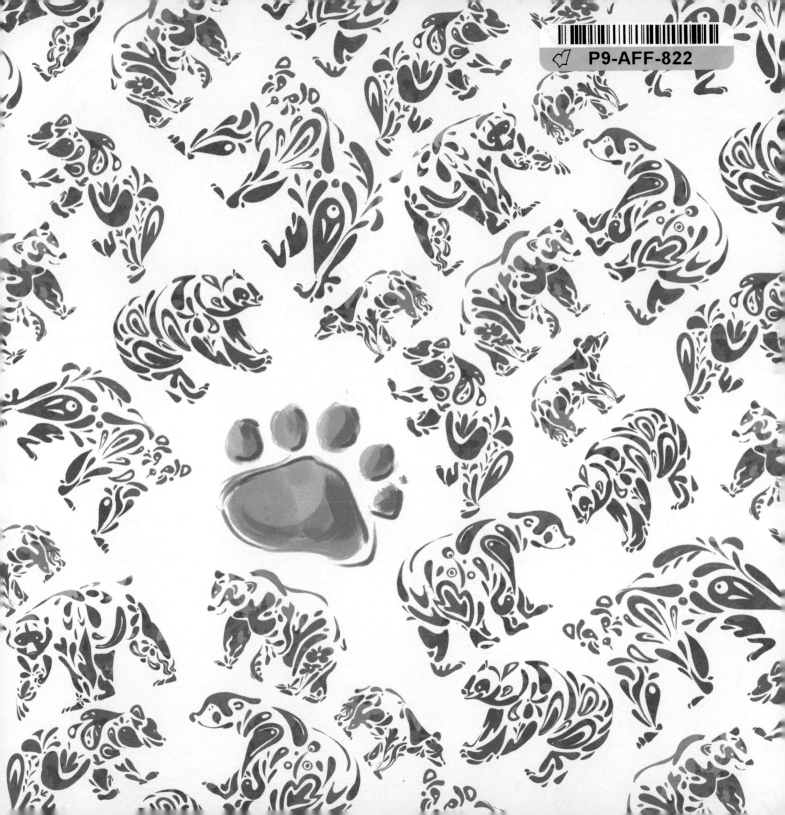

THE LIFE AND TIMES OF FUZZY WUZZY

Craig Sidell

THE LIFE
AND TIMES
OF
FUZZY WUZZY

Illustrated by Evgeniya Kozhevnikova

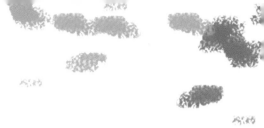

Histria Kids

Las Vegas ◊ Oxford ◊ Palm Beach

Published in the United States of America by
Histria Books, a division of Histria LLC
7181 N. Hualapai Way
Las Vegas, NV 89166 USA
HistriaBooks.com

Histria Kids is an imprint of Histria Books. Titles published under the imprints of Histria Books are distributed worldwide exclusively by the Casemate Group.

Library of Congress Control Number: 2020938698
ISBN 978-1-59211-058-2 (casebound)
Story Copyright © 2020 by Craig Sidell
Illustrations Copyright © 2020 by Histria Books

TO KATHLEEN,
CIARA,
ABIE, LENA,
JAKE,
AND NORA
FOR THEIR LIGHT
AND
ALWAYS SHINING IT BRIGHTLY.

FUZZY WUZZY WAS A BEAR

FUZZY WUZZY HAD NO HAIR

FUZZY WUZZY WASN'T FUZZY,

WAS HE?

FUZZY WAS A BEAR YOU SEE

HE WOULD CLIMB FROM TREE TO TREE

LOOKING FOR THE BEST APPLES AND PEARS

FUZZY HAD A LONG LONG LIFE
THAT HE SPENT WITH HIS FUZZY WIFE
THEY WOULD TRAVEL FAR AND NEAR

FUZZY WAS THE GREATEST DAD

SHOWING LOVE TO HIS FUZZY LAD

HE WAS A BEAR THAT REALLY CARES

FUZZY WAS A FRIEND TO ALL
GIVING HELP TO ALL WHO CALL
HIS FRIENDSHIP WAS SO VERY DEAR

FUZZY GAVE TO THOSE WHO NEED

BE IT HONEY, FRUIT, OR SEED

HE WAS A BEAR WHO ALWAYS SHARES

FUZZY SANG A FUZZY SONG
HE WOULD SING IT ALL DAY LONG
FOR THOSE LUCKY ENOUGH TO HEAR

FUZZY DANCED FROM DAWN 'TIL DUSK

HOLDING ON TO AN ELEPHANT'S TUSK

LETTING DOWN HIS NONEXISTENT HAIR

FUZZY SLEPT THE WINTER THROUGH

HE WAS A BEAR AND THAT IS TRUE

DREAMING OF ADVENTURE EVERYWHERE

FUZZY LOVED HIS FUZZY CAVE

HE REVELED IN THE WARMTH IT GAVE

KEEPING HIM SAFE THROUGHOUT THE YEAR

FUZZY WATCHED THE STARS AT NIGHT

SQUINTING EYES MADE A FUZZY LIGHT

TAKING IN THE BEAUTY THAT WAS CLEAR

FUZZY WUZZY WAS A BEAR

FUZZY WUZZY HAD NO HAIR

FUZZY WUZZY WASN'T FUZZY,

...

BUT HAD THE MOST GLORIOUS FUZZY LIFE!

ABOUT THE AUTHOR

CRAIG SIDELL GREW UP IN BEANTOWN, ATTENDED COLLEGE IN THE CITY OF BROTHERLY LOVE, AND CURRENTLY RESIDES IN THE BIG APPLE WITH HIS AMAZING WIFE AND CHILDREN. CRAIG AND HIS FAMILY ENJOY THE ENERGY AND AWESOME VEGAN FOOD IN THE CITY THAT NEVER SLEEPS. INSPIRED BY THE IMAGINATION OF HIS CHILDREN AND STEADFAST SUPPORT OF HIS FAMILY AND FRIENDS, CRAIG LOVES INVENTING STORIES AND CHARACTERS THE WHOLE WORLD CAN ENJOY.

ABOUT THE ILLUSTRATOR

EVGENIYA KOZHEVNIKOVA IS A RUSSIAN ARTIST FROM TOMSK IN SIBERIA. EVGENIYA GRADUATED FROM ART SCHOOL IN HER NATIVE CITY IN 2009. SINCE THEN, SHE HAS PAINTED MANY WATERCOLOR AND CG ILLUSTRATIONS. SHE HAS ALSO ILLUSTRATED SEVERAL CHILDREN'S BOOKS. WATERCOLOR IS HER FAVORITE MATERIAL TO WORK IN BECAUSE OF ITS UNPREDICTABILITY, ORIGINALITY, AND TEXTURE. SHE LOVES TO COMBINE HER SKILLS OF WATERCOLOR AND CG IN ORDER TO ACHIEVE A PICTURESQUE QUALITY IN EACH OF HER DRAWINGS

31901066191414